THIS BOOK BELONGS TO:

_____

_____

_____

TO MY CHILDREN, RYAN AND ANNA

YOU CAN CHANGE THE WORLD
ONE SNIPPET OF KINDNESS AT A TIME.

THIS IS A STORY ABOUT A STRANGE LITTLE PLACE,
WHERE TWO SHAPES OF PAPER FILLED UP THE WHOLE SPACE.
TRIANGLES AND SQUARES WOULD ALL WAIT IN LINE
TO MAKE A HOME IN THE SAME PATTERNED DESIGN.

EACH HOUSE LIKE THE OTHER, ALL SO MUNDANE,
NOT A CHIMNEY, A SHINGLE, OR LONG WINDOWPANE.

THEN ONE AFTERNOON, AFTER NEW SHAPES WERE MADE,
A SNIPPET SHOWED, TOO, IN AN AQUA BLUE SHADE.
BUT BECAUSE SNIPPET HAD AN ODDLY SHAPED TOP,
HE LOOKED A BIT DIFFERENT FROM A NORMAL ROOFTOP.

HE WAS VERY SHY, BUT HE WANTED TO PLAY.

SO HE ASKED THE SHAPES, "WHAT ARE YOU MAKING TODAY?"

"WE MAKE STURDY HOUSES," ANNOUNCED THE RED SQUARE.
"ASYMMETRICAL SHAPES BELONG RIGHT OVER THERE.
BECAUSE WE ARE DIFFERENT, IT'S BEST WE'RE DIVIDED.
WE JUST CAN'T RISK HAVING OUR HOUSES LOPSIDED."

SNIPPET WASN'T EXPECTING TO BE ASKED TO LEAVE,
AND WAS SHOCKED THAT SQUARE WAS BEING NAIVE.
HE COULD BUILD A STRONG HOUSE AND BE PART OF A PAIR,
EVEN THOUGH HE WAS NOT LIKE A REGULAR SQUARE.

NOT WANTING TO ARGUE, HE WALKED OVER TO THE PILE
AND NOTICED EACH SHAPE HAD A DISTINCTIVE STYLE.
THEY WERE ALL SNIPPETS! THEY WERE JUST LIKE HIM!
SOME SIDES WERE LONG, AND SOME SHAPES WERE SLIM!

HE WAS SO EXCITED BY SUCH A SURPRISE.

THERE WERE SO MANY SHAPES OF IRREGULAR SIZE.
"COME ON," THEY ALL SAID. "JUMP RIGHT INTO THE PILE."

SO SNIPPET DOVE IN WITH A BRIGHT, GLEAMING SMILE.

AND EVEN THOUGH SNIPPET REALLY LOVED THE NEW SPACE,
HE JUST COULDN'T FORGET THAT STRANGE, TIDY PLACE.
DEEP DOWN IN HIS HEART, BEING DIVIDED FELT WRONG.
HE JUST WANTED TO SEE ALL THE SHAPES GET ALONG.

AS HE STOOD THINKING, AN IDEA CAME TO MIND:
WHAT IF HE WENT BACK AND TRIED TO BE KIND...

TO THAT MISGUIDED SQUARE WITH THE PERFECT PHYSIQUE.
HE COULD SHOW HIM THE BEAUTY OF BEING UNIQUE.

WHEN SNIPPET ARRIVED, SQUARE STARTED TO GRUMBLE,
"WHY ARE YOU BACK? YOU'LL MAKE OUR HOUSES CRUMBLE."
THIS WAS SNIPPET'S BIG CHANCE TO MAKE SQUARE TRULY SEE
ALL THE WONDERFUL THINGS THEY COULD POSSIBLY BE.

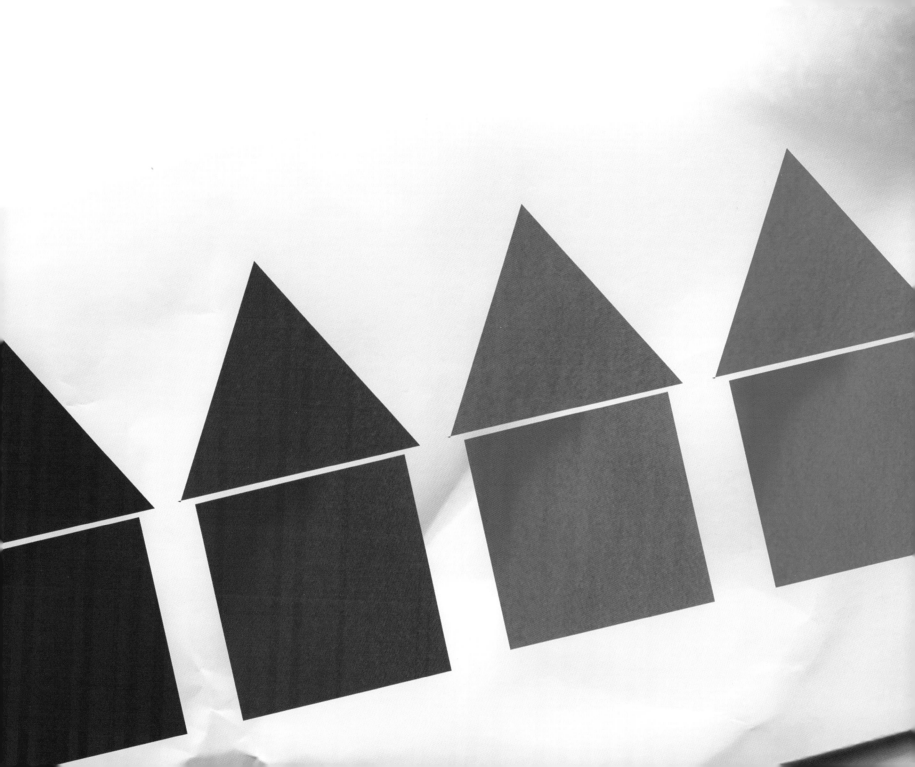

SNIPPET POINTED TO THE ROOF'S ACUTE ANGLE,
AND SAID, "I COULD MAKE A TALL CHIMNEY ON THAT GREEN TRIANGLE!"

SNIPPET SAW SQUARE START TO FILL UP WITH DOUBT.
AND KNEW IT'D BE BEST TO ACT IT ALL OUT.

SO HE CLIMBED ON THE TRIANGLE AND SAID, **"HOW'S THIS LOOK?"**

SQUARE WATCHED CAREFULLY, BUT THE HOUSE NEVER SHOOK.
"IT'S NOT FALLING DOWN, AND IT DOESN'T LOOK BAD.
IN FACT, IT LOOKS GREAT! SO, WHAT ELSE CAN WE ADD?"

"ACTUALLY," SAID SNIPPET, "WE COULD ADD SOME MORE.
THERE'S A RECTANGLE SNIPPET FOR A FANCY FRONT DOOR.
IS IT OKAY IF I ASK THE PILE TO PLAY, TOO?"
SQUARE HAPPILY AGREED, ONLY EXPECTING A FEW.
BUT THE WHOLE PILE SHOWED UP TO COME OVER AND PLAY,
AND TO SQUARE'S HUGE SURPRISE, THEY HAD SUCH A FUN DAY.

THE HOUSES THEY MADE HAD NEVER LOOKED SO GRAND.
IT WAS JUST AS WONDERFUL AS SNIPPET HAD PLANNED.
SQUARES, TRIANGLES, AND SNIPPETS ALL GETTING ALONG.
THEY'D MADE A GREAT PLACE WHERE THEY ALL COULD BELONG!

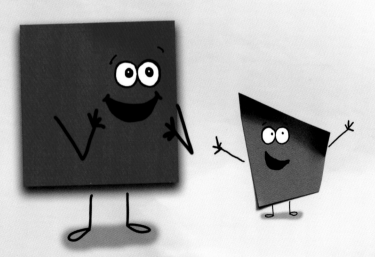

LONG RECTANGLES MADE HOUSES THAT REACHED UP SO HIGH.
A PENTAGON-SHAPED ROCKET COULD FLY IN THE SKY.
A RIGHT TRIANGLE MADE A RED SAIL ON A SHIP.
IT WAS AMAZING TO SEE SUCH CLOSE PARTNERSHIP!

THEY ALL LEARNED SO MUCH FROM EACH OTHER THAT DAY.
THAT REGARDLESS OF SHAPE, THEY COULD HAPPILY PLAY.
AND TO THINK IT WAS JUST ONE SNIPPET'S KIND HEART
THAT JOINED THEM TOGETHER TO MAKE SUCH GREAT ART.

NEXT STEPS

SHOW THE FRONT COVER OF THE BOOK AGAIN. POINT TO THE NAME OF THE AUTHOR/ILLUSTRATOR. ASK THE CHILDREN IF THEY KNOW WHAT THE AUTHOR'S AND ILLUSTRATOR'S ROLES ARE IN A BOOK. DISCUSS. DO THEY KNOW ANY OTHER NAMES OF AUTHORS AND ILLUSTRATORS?

WHO ARE THE MAIN CHARACTERS IN THIS BOOK? (SNIPPET, SQUARE.)

DISCUSS THE SHAPES WHO LIVE IN THE PAPER PLACE: WHAT DO THEY HAVE IN COMMON? (THEY ALL HAVE EQUAL SIDES AND EQUAL ANGLES.) THEY ARE CALLED "REGULAR POLYGONS." HAVE THE CHILDREN CREATE OR DRAW SOME OTHER REGULAR POLYGONS. MAKE A LIST AND LABEL THEM ACCORDING TO HOW MANY SIDES/ANGLES THEY HAVE. (EQUILATERAL TRIANGLE, RHOMBUS, SQUARE, PENTAGON, HEXAGON, SEPTAGON, OCTAGON, NONAGON, AND DECAGON.) ASK THE CHILDREN TO IDENTIFY SHAPES AROUND THEM IN THE REAL WORLD OR HAVE THEM LOOK IN MAGAZINES AND CUT OUT SHAPES. SORT THEM INTO PILES.

DISCUSS THE SHAPES IN SNIPPET'S SHAPE PILE: WHAT DO THEY HAVE IN COMMON? (THEY ALL HAVE DIFFERENT SIDE LENGTHS AND DIFFERENT ANGLES.) THEY ARE CALLED "IRREGULAR POLYGONS." HAVE THE CHILDREN CREATE OR DRAW SOME OTHER IRREGULAR POLYGONS. MAKE A LIST AND NAME THEM. (ISOSCELES TRIANGLE, RIGHT TRIANGLE, RECTANGLE, PARALLELOGRAM, TRAPEZOID, KITE, PENTAGON, HEXAGON, OCTAGON, NONAGON, DECAGON.)

COMPARE THE TWO LISTS OF POLYGONS: HOW ARE THEY THE SAME? (THEY ALL HAVE STRAIGHT SIDES THAT CONNECT. THE SIDES DON'T INTERSECT OR HAVE ANY SPACES. THEY HAVE AT LEAST THREE SIDES. THIS IS THE DEFINITION OF A "POLYGON.") HOW ARE THEY DIFFERENT? (REGULAR POLYGONS HAVE EQUAL SIDES AND EQUAL ANGLES; IRREGULAR POLYGONS DON'T.) YOU CAN ALSO DISCUSS "SYMMETRY." REGULAR POLYGONS ARE ALWAYS SYMMETRICAL. THE NUMBER OF LINES OF SYMMETRY DEPENDS ON THE NUMBER OF SIDES. SOME IRREGULAR POLYGONS HAVE LINES OF SYMMETRY, AND SOME DON'T.

WHY DOESN'T SQUARE WANT SNIPPET TO BE IN THE PAPER PLACE? WHY DOES SNIPPET REALLY WANT TO BE A PART OF THE PAPER PLACE? HAVE THE CHILDREN EVER WANTED TO BE A PART OF SOMETHING FROM WHICH THEY ARE KEPT OUT? DISCUSS. HOW DID IT MAKE THEM FEEL?

ASK THE CHILDREN HOW SQUARE FEELS AT THE BEGINNING OF THE BOOK. AT THE END? WHAT CHANGES HIM? SQUARE JUST WANTS THINGS TO STAY THE SAME. HE IS SCARED TO TRY SOMETHING NEW. ASK THE CHILDREN IF THIS EVER HAPPENED TO THEM. WHEN HAS TRYING SOMETHING NEW ENDED UP BEING A GOOD THING?

HAVE THE CHILDREN NAME THEIR FAVORITE NEW "CREATION" THE REGULAR AND IRREGULAR POLYGONS MADE AT THE END OF THE BOOK. EITHER GIVE THE CHILDREN CUTOUTS OF DIFFERENT SHAPES, OR HAVE THEM MAKE THEIR OWN. LET THEM CREATE SOMETHING WITH THEM (MAYBE GLUE THEM DOWN ON CONSTRUCTION PAPER). WHEN THEY'RE DONE, HAVE THEM HOLD UP THEIR CREATIONS AND DISCUSS HOW THE CREATIONS ARE ALL UNIQUE, JUST AS THE CHILDREN ARE.